Annabel

Story by Joy Cowley
Illustrations by Kathleen McCord

There once was a girl called Annabel.
There once was a girl called Annabel.
Anna, Anna, bel, bel, bel.
Anna, Anna, bel, bel, bel.
There once was a girl called Annabel.

She went out shopping with her crocodile.
She went out shopping with her crocodile.
Croco, croco, dile, dile, dile.
Croco, croco, dile, dile, dile.
She went out shopping with her crocodile.

She bought a bottle of pink shampoo.
She bought a bottle of pink shampoo.
Pink sham, pink sham, poo, poo, poo.
Pink sham, pink sham, poo, poo, poo.
She bought a bottle of pink shampoo.

The crocodile wanted a new toothbrush.
The crocodile wanted a new toothbrush.
New tooth, new tooth, brush, brush, brush.
New tooth, new tooth, brush, brush, brush.
The crocodile wanted a new toothbrush.

The people in the shop were terrified.
The people in the shop were terrified.
Terri, terri, fied, fied, fied.
Terri, terri, fied, fied, fied.
The people in the shop were terrified.

Annabel said, "We'd better go."
Annabel said, "We'd better go.
Better, better, go, go, go.
Better, better, go, go, go."
Annabel said, "We'd better go."

They got on a train for Baltimore.
They got on a train for Baltimore.
Balti, Balti, more, more, more.
Balti, Balti, more, more, more.
They got on a train for Baltimore.

If you want any more, just start again.
If you want any more, just start again.
Start a, start a, gain, gain, gain.
Start a, start a, gain, gain, gain.
If you want any more, just start again.